THAT FRUIT IS MINE!

ANUSKA ALLEPUZ

WALKER BOOKS
AND SUBSIDIARIES
LONDON • BOSTON • SYDNEY • AUCKLAND

Deep in the heart of the jungle,
lived five elephants.

In that jungle grew lots of fruit.
The elephants LOVED fruit.

Elephant One
munched on mangoes.

Elephant Two
craved coconuts.

Elephant Three
was keen on kiwis.

Elephant Four
banqueted on bananas.

And **Elephant Five**
preferred pineapples.

But one day, deep, *deep* in the heart
of the jungle, the elephants discovered
a new tree. A new, very TALL tree.

And on that very tall tree was the MOST delicious-looking exotic fruit that the elephants had ever seen.

EVERYONE wanted to eat it.

Hey, look at THAT!

"MINE!"

cried Elephant One.

"That fruit is MINE!"

She KNEW that she could reach it.
She *huffed* and she *puffed*
with all her might...

One,
two,
three,
four,
five.
Up,
up,
up!

PFFFT!

The fruit didn't move an itty bitty inch.

Heave
ho!
One,
two,
three,
four,
five.
Up,
up,
up!

"MINE!"
said Elephant Two.
"That fruit is MINE!"

She KNEW that she had a very smart idea. She could already taste that sweet, sweet fruit...

Keep stretching!

Look! A humongous bug!

HMPH!

Hmmm, perhaps her idea
needed a little more work.

"MINE!"

shouted Elephant Three.
"That fruit is MINE!"
He KNEW that he was cleverer
than Elephant One and Elephant Two.
So, with a he-e-e-eave
and a stre-e-e-etch,
he started to climb...

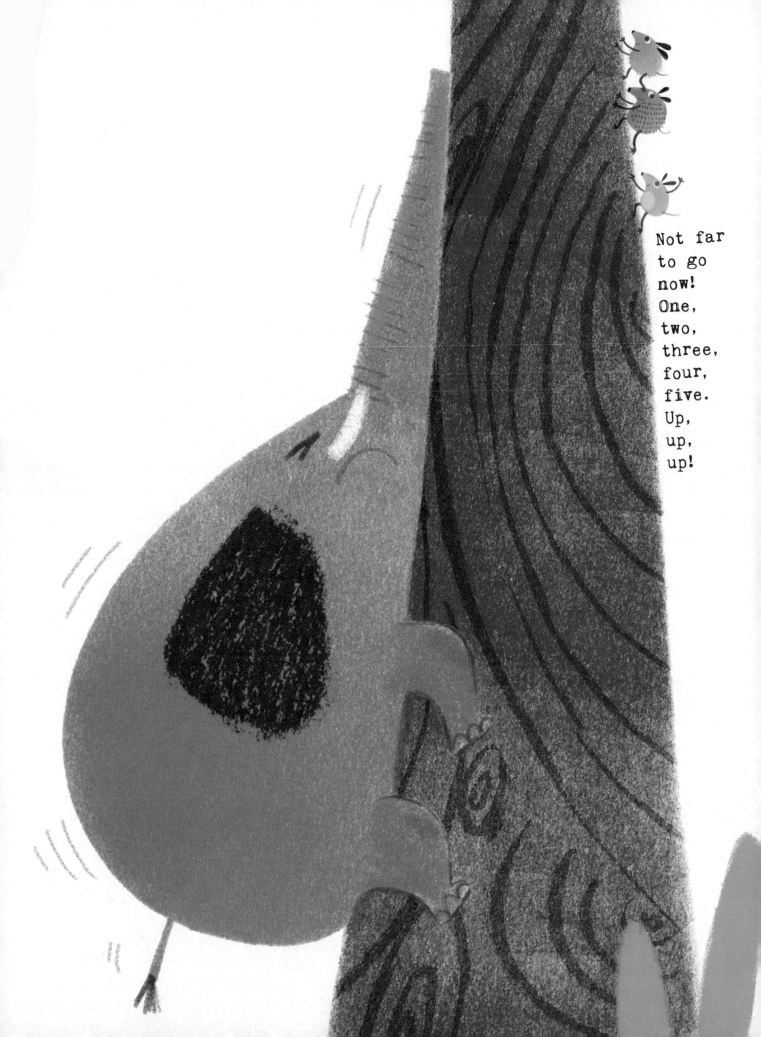

Not far
to go
now!
One,
two,
three,
four,
five.
Up,
up,
up!

OOF!

He didn't get very far at all.

I can almost reeeeeeach!

The elephants were getting VERY impatient and VERY hungry! Elephant Four decided to just run at the tree as fast as he could.

"MINE!"

"MINE!"

said the elephants, all at once.
But just at that moment ...

the delicious-looking exotic fruit began ...

Now the delicious-looking exotic fruit belonged
to the five mice, who carried it ... TOGETHER!
"This fruit is OURS!" the five mice said.

The elephants looked on, astonished.

"OURS?"

said the elephants.

Hooray!
We've got
the fruit!

"OURS!"

said the elephants, all at once.

"Why didn't *we* think of that!?"

Huff!

Puff!

"OURS!"

Huff!

He-e-e-e^av_e!

"OURS!"
Stre-e-e-etch!

"This fruit is OURS!"

And that's how, deep, *deep* in the heart
of the jungle, the elephants finally got
their delicious-looking exotic fruit.

"Weren't there
five of us?"

"OURS!"

Thank you most of all to Mum and my brother Alberto.

Thank you to Martin Salisbury, Alexis Deacon, Anne-Louise Jones, Maria Tunney and Helen Mackenzie-Smith.

Thank you all for making it possible for me to create this book, my first picture book!